The Fox and the Hedgehog

Written by Valerie L. Pate

Illustrated by Penny Barron

Dedicated to hedgehog rescue shelters everywhere; including our very own local service, which is kindly provided by a true animal hero (Lorraine at Hull Hedgehog Hospital, Anlaby Road). Remember, if you see a hedgehog out in the daytime, they are in need of assistance; most likely hungry and dehydrated. To locate your nearest shelter go to www.helpwildlife.co.uk

In a slice of silver moonlight, the fox sat tall and silent.
The night air stirred and her ears gave a twitch.

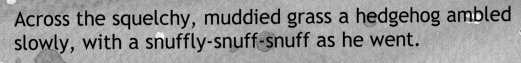

Across the squelchy, muddied grass a hedgehog ambled slowly, with a snuffly-snuff-snuff as he went.

The hedgehog was searching for earth worms.

The fox was also hungry.

In her shadowy stillness, the fox was nearly invisible.

The hedgehog, lying low on the ground and mostly unaware, caught the fox's eye.

The fox flicked her tail.

With a start, the hedgehog instantly rolled himself into a ball with a great kerfuffle of snuffles and spines.

The trifling, little hedgehog was paralysed with fear and could hardly catch his breath.

Foxes were not friends of hedgehogs!

The fox didn't fancy a mouthful of spines and she hadn't the appetite for making sport with the poor creature.

What she wanted was a meal.

The hedgehog peeked through his bristles at the regal, red stranger sitting still and straight in the shadows.

.

The hedgehog couldn't imagine why she was waiting. He didn't dare hope that she was actually planning to let him escape.

"Tell me, young hedgehog, have you seen any rabbits about?" the fox questioned faintly.

"Rabbits?" the hedgehog squeaked.

"Yes, rabbits," she replied impatiently. "They have long ears and hop about."

"Of course, they do, of course," the hedgehog snuffled fearfully. "I know of rabbits."

He unfurled himself slightly and regarded the fox warily.

Her luminous eyes were intently boring down upon him.

"Have you seen any about this night?"

"Uh...yes," he stammered. "By the barn. There were a couple feeding there when I was passing."

The fox nodded her head and stood, noting how her movements caused the anxious hedgehog to tremble.

There was a flash of red as she darted out of sight.

"Good night, young hedgehog," her low voice lilted.

It was several days later when the hedgehog noticed the fox drinking from a puddle in the blue glint of twilight.

He was just licking the last few morsels of his evening meal from the corners of his mouth as he was shuffling along, when the fox came into view.

He stifled a squeal but ended up sneezing!

"Young hedgehog," said the fox, almost fondly, "you best not linger near the roadway. Surely you know what befalls creatures who make *that* mistake."

The hedgehog shambled towards the safety of the brush as quickly as he could. "Yes, Mistress Fox," he replied, "I do indeed know of the roaring glow-eyed monsters that the humans tame and ride. They do frighten me out of my very wits, Mistress."

"Come this way then and I'll show you a much safer place to cross," the fox beckoned.

Her smile seemed sincere but the hedgehog had heard many tales of slickly sly foxes.

The hedgehog hesitated, snuffling most fretfully and causing the fox to almost pity him.

"Do come, young hedgehog. I promise not to bite."

The hedgehog did not care to hear the word 'bite' uttered aloud at that moment, but it was a fact that the fox had spared him before.

He lumbered along in her wake, noticing the way her paws tread upon the grass with such delicate grace.

A fog had settled upon the ground and the young hedgehog found fox most frightfully beautiful: all wrapped in misty vapours.

"This is the path for you, my young friend," said Mistress Fox, indicating a small tunnel that led through the hedgerow and onto the farmer's fields. "Some birds were feasting upon worms there just this morning."

The hedgehog was stunned by the fox's kindness, but managed to utter his thanks.

As the fox turned to go, the young hedgehog mustered his courage and daringly questioned, "Why have you been so pleasant to me, good Mistress?"

The Fox cocked her head and regarded the funny little animal before her.

"I do not enjoy having my tongue prickled," she explained at last, "and I feel it's impolite to needlessly frighten a creature which I don't intend to eat."

The hedgehog realised that his aquaintance was no ordinary sort of fox.

His anxiety subsided and he bowed his head in thanks.

Then, as before, the fox was gone.

As the darkening days passed, the fox and hedgehog continued to cross paths on occasion.

They would regard each other with courtesy and respect, much to the perplexity of the other animals around them.

The young hedgehog's kin gaped in wonder at the majestic fox that never once chased or pawed them; so that every once in a while she would show them her teeth with a menacing grin, to to keep them on their guard.

One autumn evening when the ground was a carpet of crunchng, rust coloured leaves, the hedgehog was using his snout to stuff an old rotting log with some soft, mossy bedding.

"Have you seen any rabbits about?" the fox called to him softly, a smile in her tone.

"Ah, Mistress Fox," the busy hedgehog replied, "I have been occupied with making my winter bed this evening and so have not observed many goings-on at all, I must say."

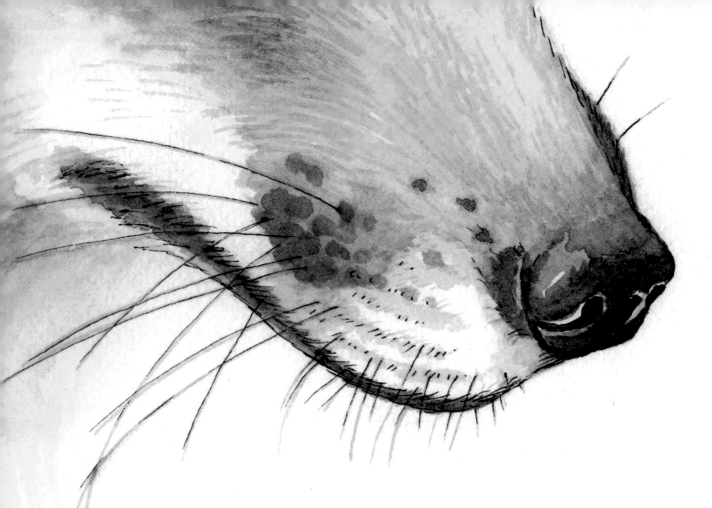

The fox considered the hedgehog for a moment, her whiskers quivering ever so slightly in the breeze. She recalled that many small creatures slumbered the cold months away, rather than starve when the world became bleak.

"Are you very tired then, young hedgehog?"

The hedgehog yawned, as if to illustrate his fatigue and nodded.

"I am due for a very long sleep, Mistress Fox. I only hope that I have chosen a safe enough place to take my rest."

The fox's ears swivelled and she bowed her head down low, so that she was level with the hedgehog's dark, beady eyes.

"I will pass here often and look out for you," she told him with a gentle sincerity. "Rest well, young hedgehog and when you awaken you will be fully grown."

The hedgehog was profoundly warmed and comforted by the fox's unexpected vow.

He slowly ducked his head one last time, his eyes unwaveringly meeting the fox's level gaze, before retreating into the old log's freshly padded hollow.

"Goodnight Mistress Fox," he murmured as he peacefully drifted down into his winter slumber.

A gentle breeze blew through the bare branches, as the fox sat alone, tall and regal in the shadows beside the old, rotting log.

Her coat glowed silver in a beam of crescent moonlight. She sat so still and silent that she was very nearly invisible.

"Goodnight," she whispered; and her words were taken by the wind and scattered like rust-coloured leaves that swirled beneath the stars.

Valerie L. Pate began writing poems and stories at a very young age. In recent years she has focused her creative energies upon children's stories and greatly enjoys encouraging young people to interact with nature and appreciate our environment.

Valerie and her husband, Adam, have two daughters, a white cat and a bearded dragon. Her most favourite season is autumn.

You can follow Valerie on Facebook at www.facebook.com/VPWriter

Penny Barron has lived and worked in the East Riding for all her life. Her love of art and nature has provided a wealth of subject matter for the watercolour and pastel paintings she creates. She exhibits locally and as an art teacher she hopes to pass on her enthusiasm and experience to young and old.

'Illustrating children's books is like the cherry on the top of a delicious, creative cake!'

Made in the USA
Middletown, DE
17 October 2016